ISBN 0-439-74339-7

12 11 10 9 8 7 6 5 4 3 2                    5 6 7 8 9 10/0

Printed in Singapore                                        46

First Scholastic printing, January 2005

The illustrations in this book were done in Adobe Illustrator.
Designed by Scott Piehl

# OLIVE MY LOVE

Written by
## VIVIAN WALSH

Illustrated by
## J.OTTO SEIBOLD

SCHOLASTIC INC.
New York  Toronto  London  Auckland  Sydney
Mexico City  New Delhi  Hong Kong  Buenos Aires

OLIVE,

To Cecilia,
which rhymes with Amelia,
ALL OF my love —V. W.

For T., A., and U. —J.o. S.

my LOVE

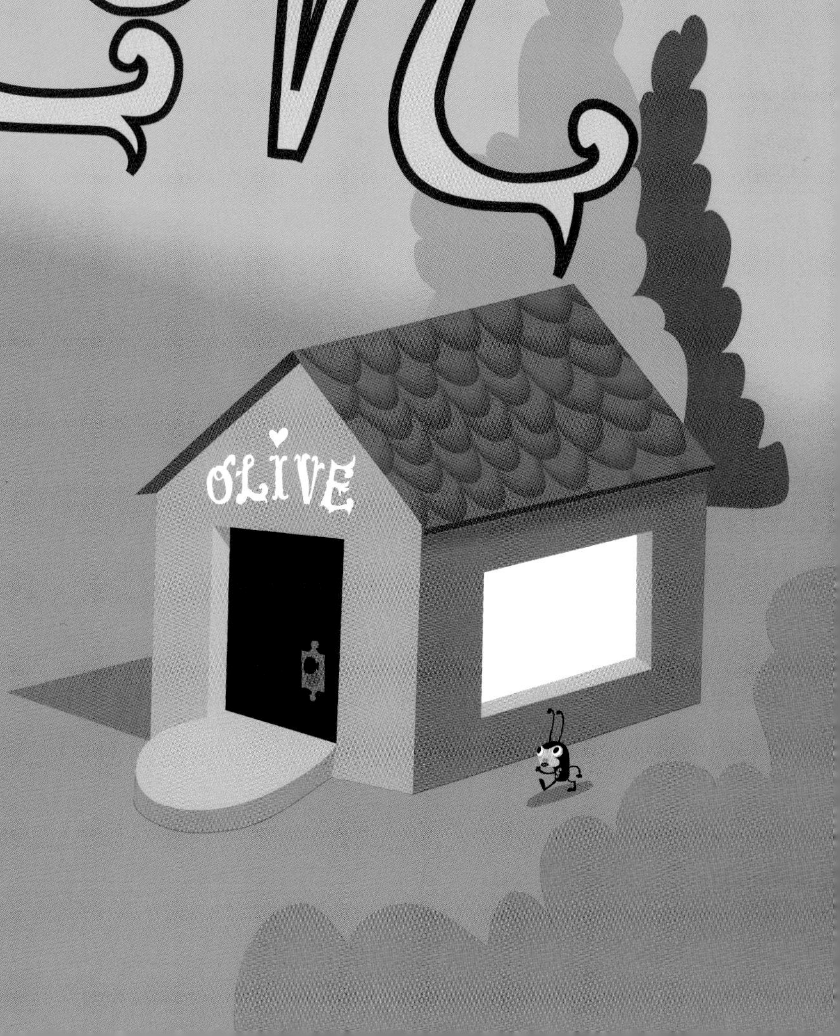

One afternoon,
Olive was baking her favorite treat,
dog biscuits.

Baking made Olive's kitchen feel warm and smell sweet.

When the biscuits were done, Olive lay down in a sunny
spot to take a nap.

"Now I feel warm and sweet, too," thought Olive.

She was nearly asleep when she thought she heard someone
calling her name.

She perked up her ears and listened.
Someone was singing.

**"... my love to you."**

"Ah woo," Olive sang along.
It is something dogs have to do.

It was her friend Dexter, the winged dog.
"A dog with wings that sings," thought Olive.
"I like that."

He was singing really loud now.

**"All of my love,
all of my love ..."**

Olive sang, too. She tipped back her head,
and when Dexter sang the last words—

**"... to you."**

—she howled, "Ah woooo."

The song was interrupted by a—

**THUMP!**

Olive jumped up. The fur on her back jumped up, too.

On Olive's doorstep was the biggest heart she had ever seen. "You dropped all of your love!" Olive called out. But it was too late. Dexter had already flown away.

"I'd better return it," thought Olive.

She filled a sack with fresh biscuits.
When you're going on an adventure,
it's good to pack a snack.

Olive hadn't gone far when she heard these four words:

"Stop! No! Don't go!"

Olive stopped.

"Stand clear of the rut!" instructed a squirrel.

Just then, down the rut rolled a nut.

The squirrel held it up to show Olive.

"Now I can say hello.
Hello! My name is Handler.
I have more nuts than any
other squirrel on the hill.
They fall off the tree,
roll into my rut,
and that's a one-way trip to
where I want them to be.
I don't have to go gather nuts; nuts come to me.
And I'm soooo pleased to meet you."
(The squirrel could talk really fast.)

"What do you do with so many nuts?" asked Olive.

"I count them. One, two, three, four, five, six . . . phew!
Sometimes it takes all day to count them," said Handler.
"Want to help?"

"I'd love to stay and count with you," said Olive,
"but I have to return this heart."

"Oh, let me count that for you: ONE.
You have ONE heart," said Handler, looking very pleased
with himself. He picked up a bunch of nuts and hugged
them.

"This is Dexter's heart," said Olive.
"He lost it."

"Oh," said Handler, letting a few nuts fall from his grip,
"you'd better return that. To you, I say:
Good luck and good-bye."

Olive pushed the heart.

Olive pulled the heart.

This was hard work.
Olive was tired.

She decided it was time to reward herself with a treat.
As she chewed on her biscuit, she heard a voice say:

"Eight, nine, and ten!"
It was Handler. Olive had hardly moved.
Dexter's heart was really big.

"Handler, do you know a horse or a mule who lives nearby?
Some kind of an animal that can carry something big?"
said Olive. "An elephant would be good."

Handler didn't feel like counting nuts anymore. He felt like
helping Olive.

"We could take my car," said Handler.

"Which way?" asked Handler.

"Ruff," said Olive, sniffing the air.
Olive pointed the way. It's something dogs can do.

Olive liked to ride in cars.

She loved to sit by the window.

They drove up the hill.
Olive could see Dexter's house.

"It's just on the other side of that cliff," Handler said.

**"Cliff!?"** Olive yelped.

"Stop. No! Handler, don't go!"

Handler hit the brakes. The car jerked to a stop.

The heart, not knowing any better, kept going.

It shot forward toward the cliff.
And then it froze in midair.

It was caught in some kind of net.

"What is that in my web?" asked a spider.

"It's Dexter's heart," said Olive. "He lost it."

"Oh," said the spider, "you'd better return that."

"We're trying to," said Handler. "Can we drive there?"

"Impossible! No car can make it across the steep ravine. Even Dexter can't drive to his house—he flies. I wonder if I can help. My name is Weaver."

Weaver began to wind silk thread around some branches. "Weaving helps me think," she explained. She made a hammock. "Swinging in a hammock helps me think, too."

Olive thought for a while, and then she said,
"A treat helps me think." She opened her sack of biscuits.

Handler had brought some treats, too.
"Would anyone like a nut chew?" asked the squirrel.

"Oh, *ah chooo!*" said the spider, sneezing.
"I'm allergic to nut chews. Would either of you like
a fly wing?"

Oddly enough, both Olive and Handler were allergic to
fly wings.

"FLY WINGS!" said Weaver. "That's it! Flying!"

She turned her hammock over and stretched it back.
"A slingshot can ka-bolt you over the ravine.
You can fly to Dexter's house!"

"Only a very brave dog could do that," said Handler.

Olive looked at the heart and thought about her friend
Dexter, the dog with wings that sings.

Olive was a brave dog.

One, Two,

**Off She Flew!**

Dexter opened his door and saw a huge heart lying there.

"I've brought your heart back!" said Olive.

"My heart?" asked Dexter.

"You lost it. You were singing, 'All of my love . . . ,'" said Olive.

"I didn't lose my heart, Olive. I gave it to you," said Dexter. "Didn't you get my note?"

"Note? Nope." Olive was confused. She was staring at a piece of paper stuck on Dexter's wing. It was the note. Dexter sang the words that he had written there.

## FOR OLIVE,
### MY LOVE,
### ALL OF MY LOVE.
#### YOURS, DEXTER

"The heart is a gift for me?" asked Olive.

"For you?!" sang a voice. It was Handler.

"We tagged along!" said Weaver. "We're still attached."

She held up a strand that connected them to the heart.

Dexter helped Olive open the heart.
There were bonbons inside.

"What a sweet mistake!" said Handler.

The new friends had a picnic of bonbons, biscuits, nut chews, and fly wings. They were surprised they had so much to share with one another.

They felt happy on top of the hill.

They felt like they were on top of the world.